SASSAFRAS

by Audrey Penn

Illustrated by Ruth E. Harper

SCHOLASTIC INC.
New York Toronto London Auckland Sydney

ISBN 0-590-04703-5

Copyright © 1995 by Child Welfare League of America, Inc. All rights reserved.
Published by Scholastic Inc., 555 Broadway, New York, NY 10012,
by arrangement with Child & Family Press,
an imprint of the Child Welfare League of America, Inc.
SCHOLASTIC and associated logos are trademarks and/or registered
trademarks of Scholastic Inc.

12 11 10 9 8 7 6 5 4 3 2 1   8 9/9 0 1 2 3/0

Printed in the U.S.A.   24

First Scholastic printing, November 1998

Book design by S. Dmitri Lipczenko
Production by Hannah Kleber, Rockville, MD

Sassafras hid in the hollow
of a big oak tree.

"I hope nobody finds me," sighed the sad little skunk.
"I hope no one is looking."

"There you are, Sassafras!" squealed Porcupine.
He poked his spiny head into the log and blinked
in the darkness. "Whatcha doin' in there?"

"Hiding," said the skunk.

Gray Squirrel ran across the top of
the log. "Well, come on out," he called.
"Let's go run in the leaves."

"You don't want to play with me," said
Sassafras, slipping further into the hollow tree.
"I might... you know... make a bit of a stink."

"Too true. Too true," sniffed Screech Owl. She sat high above the others, always on the lookout for danger. "That little skunk can make an awful big smell."

"We don't mind, do we, Gray Squirrel?" said Porcupine. "We just want him to play." But the shy little skunk just lowered his head and said nothing.

When Porcupine and Gray
Squirrel left, Sassafras climbed
out of the log and walked to
the edge of Willow Pond.

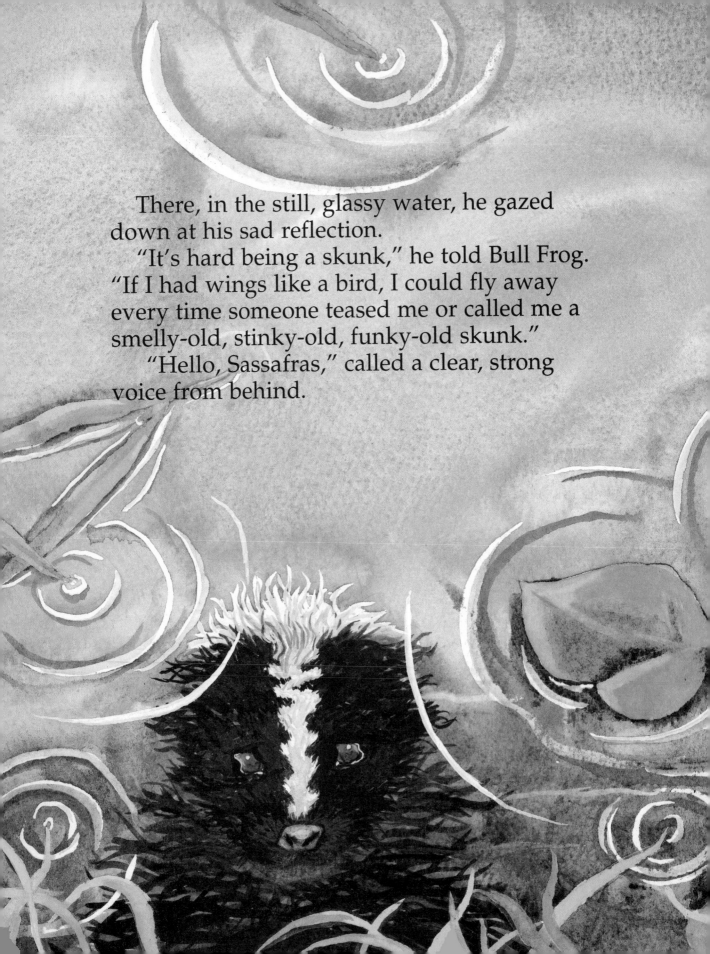

There, in the still, glassy water, he gazed down at his sad reflection.

"It's hard being a skunk," he told Bull Frog. "If I had wings like a bird, I could fly away every time someone teased me or called me a smelly-old, stinky-old, funky-old skunk."

"Hello, Sassafras," called a clear, strong voice from behind.

Sassafras turned around. "Hello, Poppy! You smell like root beer!"

The wise old skunk chuckled. "That's not me," said Poppy. "I'm chewing sassafras root. Sassafras root is sweet—like you!"

"Aw, I'm not sweet," said Sassafras with a blush. "Sassafras is just my name."

Poppy put down the piece of tasty tree root and joined Sassafras by the pond.

"What are you doing here by yourself?" Poppy asked gently. "Your friends are running in the field."

"Nothing much," sighed Sassafras. "I'm trying not to stink up the woods."

"Oh... I see." Poppy's coal black eyes twinkled in the morning light. "I used to worry about that very same thing when I was a young skunk," he told Sassafras. "But a skunk is a skunk. We are who we're meant to be. That stink is part of being a skunk, like the stinger is part of a bee."

"Ouch!" squealed Sassafras. "Nobody likes bees!"

"That's not true!" said Poppy. "Bees help the flowers and make sweet honey. It's their stingers nobody likes."

"Well, around here," said the young skunk,
"it's the stink nobody likes."

"Every animal in the forest has some special way of helping it stay safe," explained Poppy. "Some animals blend in with the forest. Some animals are big and strong. Some have teeth and claws."

Poppy looked at Sassafras with pride. "Birds have wings. Bees have stingers. Porcupines have quills. And skunks have smelly-old, stinky-old, funky-old spray."

Poppy was about
to say more when
Screech Owl
sounded a sudden
alarm, bringing all
the animals together.
"There's a stranger
coming," she called
to her friends.
"Quickly, quickly!
Everyone hide!"

Gray Squirrel ran to the end of a
tree branch and threw acorns into
the underbrush.

Porcupine scurried up a tree,
shook loose several long, spiny quills,
and sent them sailing down below.

And Sassafras stamped his foot and snarled at the sound of rustling leaves.

But when the sounds grew closer, the brave little
skunk turned his back to the noise, raised his thick,
bushy tail straight into the air, and sprayed two
yellow streams of skunk oil.

"Bull's-eye!" cheered Sassafras, quickly moving
away. "That should send them running."

But instead, the woods grew still and quiet.

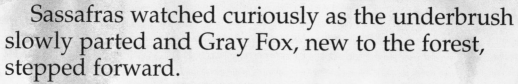

Sassafras watched curiously as the underbrush slowly parted and Gray Fox, new to the forest, stepped forward.

Gray Fox crinkled her nose at the skunk smell, plucked the stinging quill from her tail, and rubbed her head where Gray Squirrel's acorn had hit.

"Gosh," she sighed. "I only
wanted to play." And with a slow,
sad turn and a drooping head,
she started to walk away.

"Please don't go!" called Sassafras. He waddled toward the fox and put his soft gentle paw near hers. "We're sorry. We didn't mean to frighten you, but we didn't know who you were."

"I know," whispered Gray Fox. "I'm not bright and pretty and easy to see like Red Fox. And I don't make loud noises."

"I think your fur is beautiful," said Sassafras. "And Poppy says your gray fur and quiet ways help you blend into the woods and keep you safe. All of us have some special way of staying safe," he proudly explained. "Bees have stingers. Porcupines have quills...."

"And skunks," yelled everyone else, "have smelly-old, stinky-old, funky-old spray."

"You know," said Sassafras, as he and his friends led Gray Fox toward Willow Pond,

"we are who we are. That's the way it should be.
Even smelly-old, stinky-old, funky-old me!"